How Do Dinosaurs Eat Their Food?

DEINONYCHUS

PROTOCERATOPS

LAMBEOSAURUS

POLACANTHUS

AMARGASAURUS

GORGOSAURUS

CRYOLOPHOSAURUS

SPINOSAURUS

SUPERSAURUS

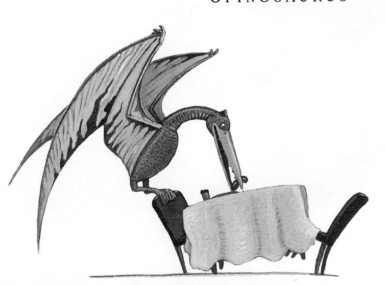

QUETZALCOATLUS

DEINONYCHUS

PROTOCERATOPS

LAMBEOSAURUS

POLACANTHUS

AMARGASAURUS

GORGOSAURUS

CRYOLOPHOSAURUS

SPINOSAURUS

SUPERSAURUS

QUETZALCOATLUS

JANE YOLEN

How Do Dinosaurs

Eat Their Food?

Illustrated by

MARK TEAGUE

SCHOLASTIC INC.
New York Toronto London Auckland
Sydney New Delhi Hong Kong

This book was originally published in hardcover by the Blue Sky Press in 2005.

ISBN-13: 978-0-545-24074-1

ISBN-10: 0-545-24074-3

Text copyright © 2005 by Jane Yolen.

Illustrations copyright © 2005 by Mark Teague.

2 3 4 5 6 7 8 9 10   08   18 17 16 15 14 13 12 11 10 09

Printed in the U.S.A.

First Scholastic paperback printing, September 2006

To wee David, who is a splendid dinosaur

J. Y.

For Michael Cavanaugh

M. T.

How does a dinosaur
eat all his food?
Does he burp,
does he belch,
or make noises
quite rude?

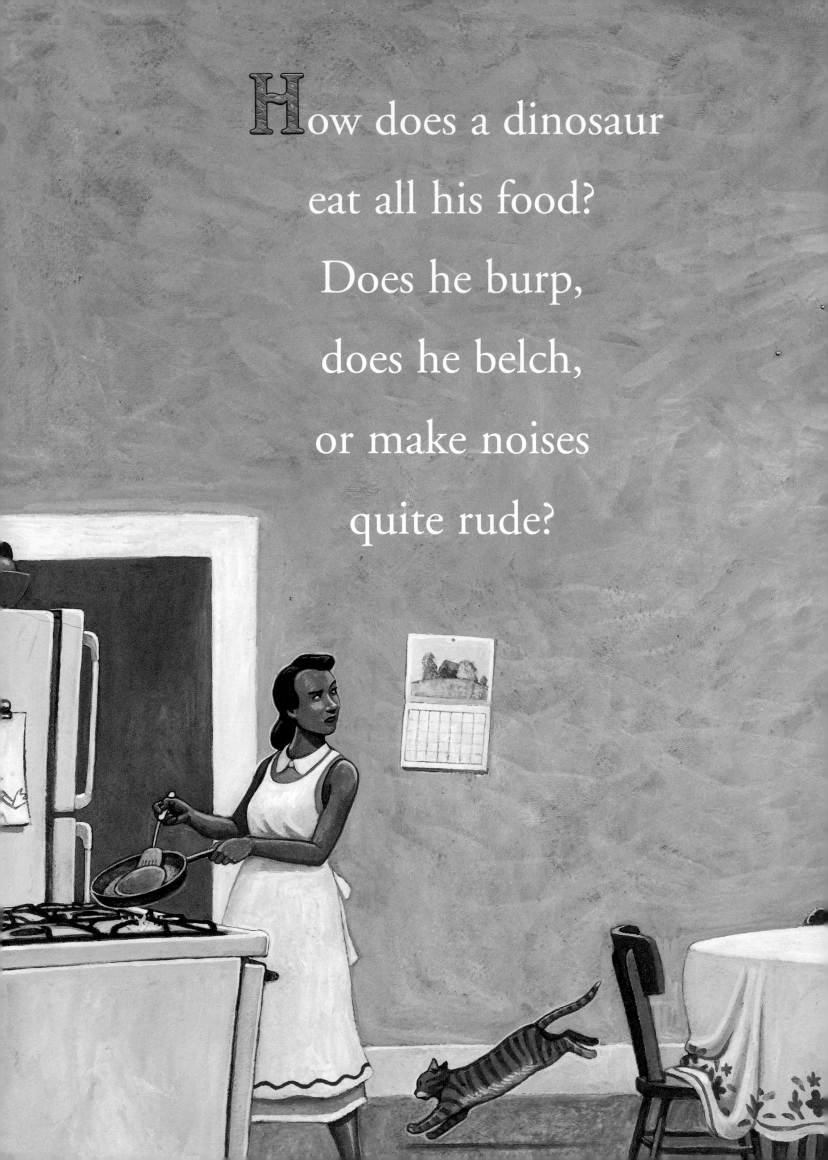

CRYOLOPHOSAURUS

Does he pick at his cereal, throw down

his cup,

hoping to make someone else pick it up?

Does he fuss, does he fidget,
or squirm in his chair?

Does he flip his spaghetti

high into the air?

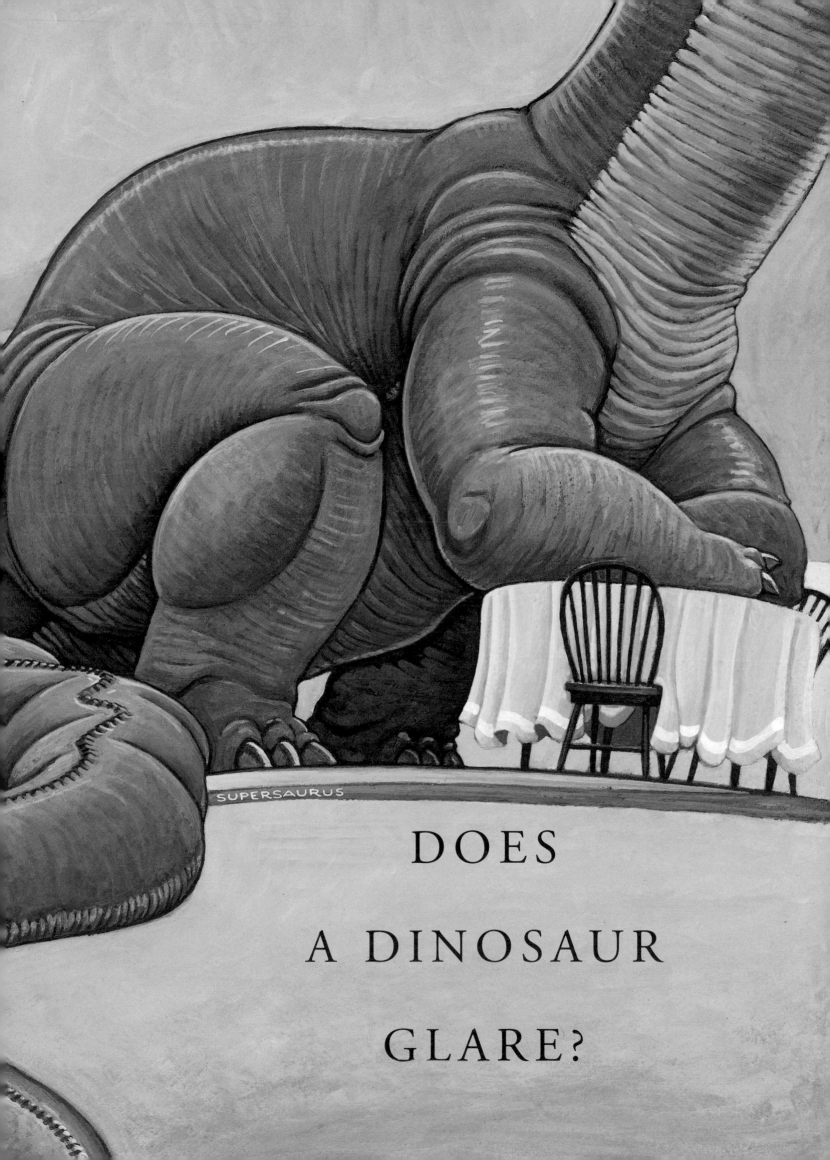

DOES

A DINOSAUR

GLARE?

How does a dinosaur
eat all his food?
Does he spit
out his broccoli
partially chewed?

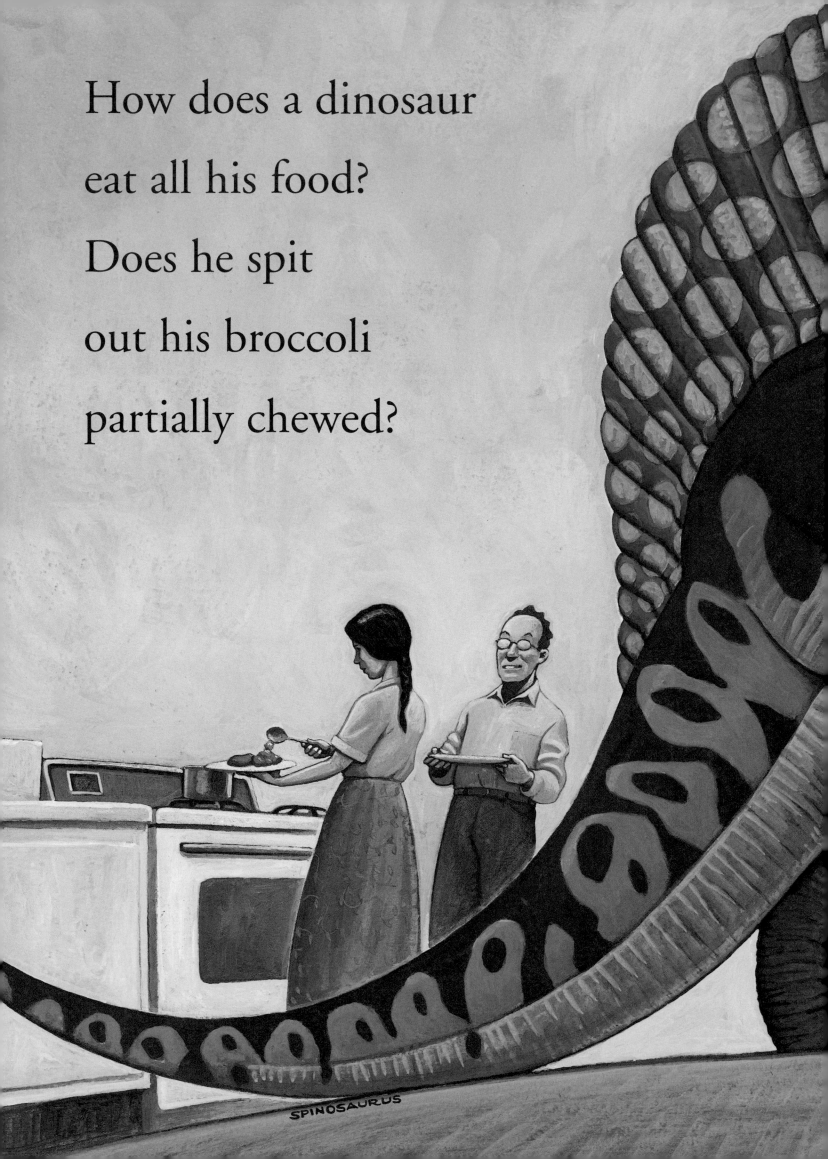

Does he bubble

his milk?

Stick beans

up his nose?

GORGOSAURUS

Does he squeeze juicy oranges
with his big toes?

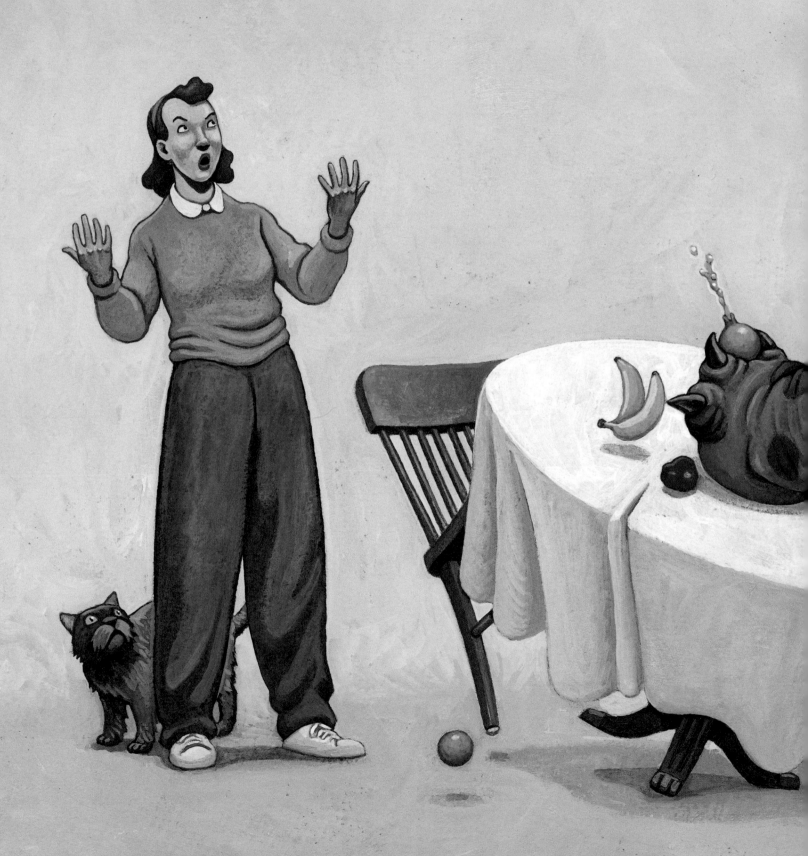

POLACANTHUS

No . . .

He says, "Please"

and "Thank you."
He sits very still.

He eats all before him
with smiles and goodwill.

He tries
every new thing,
at least one
small bite.

He makes
no loud noises—
that isn't polite.

He never
drops anything
onto the floor.
And after
he's finished,
he asks for
some more.

Eat up.

Eat up, little dinosaur.

DEINONYCHUS

PROTOCERATOPS

LAMBEOSAURUS

POLACANTHUS

AMARGASAURUS

CRYOLOPHOSAURUS

SPINOSAURUS

GORGOSAURUS

SUPERSAURUS

QUETZALCOATLUS

DEINONYCHUS

PROTOCERATOPS

LAMBEOSAURUS

POLACANTHUS

AMARGASAURUS

CRYOLOPHOSAURUS

SPINOSAURUS

GORGOSAURUS

SUPERSAURUS

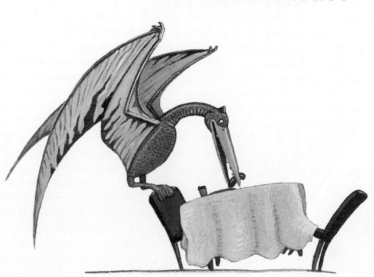

QUETZALCOATLUS